By MARY and CONRAD BUFF

HOUGHTON MIFFLIN COMPANY BOSTON

ISBN: 0-395-18591-2 REINFORCED EDITION

Ninth Printing v

PROLOGUE

Many many years past,
Over six hundred years ago
In the year twelve hundred and ninety,
Thirty-three men on a mountain meadow
Gathered together at midnight.

Peaceful men,
Herders of cattle,
Hunters of chamois,
Skilled with the crossbow.

From different cantons they came,
Some hailed from Uri,
Others from Schwzy,
Still others from Underwalden.

And on that moonless night
Over six hundred years ago,
Thirty-three men talked long
Seeking an answer for freedom,
Seeking an answer for peace.

Thirty-three men on a mountain meadow
Many many years ago.

1

A Promise

"MISSED it again. Go find the arrow, Rudi. It fell near that old rotten log over there. The one with the big hole in it."

Walter Tell laid his Swiss crossbow on the grass and sat down on a granite rock in the green Alpine pasture. He stared at the white circles he had carved on a big pine tree, the target at which he had shot all afternoon.

"Will I ever, ever hit the bull's-eye?" he asked himself. "Will I ever become a great bowman like Father when I grow up?"

Little Rudi, his brother, and Prinz, the herd dog, scrambled about in the pine forest searching for the lost arrow. As he waited for them to find it, Walter glanced up at the cold gray peaks of the Alps, white with autumn snow.

"Here it is. Prinz smelled it," shouted Rudi, holding up the arrow in his little brown hand and smiling happily. Prinz barked and wagged his tail. He always barked when he found an arrow. He seemed to know that his nose was keener than even Rudi's sharp blue eyes. "It was under the ferns by that rotten log," laughed Rudi, as he handed the arrow to his brother. "Try again, Walter, maybe this time you will hit it."

"There's the evening bell, Rudi. But I'll shoot once more. Then we must go home for the goats are getting restless and the wind is chilly." The goats, feeling the oncoming night, were already nibbling their way downward.

Standing with his legs apart, Walter placed an arrow in his crossbow and drew back the leather thong. Then sighting the target he suddenly unlatched the trigger. "Twang," sped the arrow. To his utter surprise, Walter saw it bury itself in the very center of the target.

"You hit it! You hit it!" shouted Rudi, jumping up and down in happiness. "If Father would only come now and see."

Walter eyed the quivering arrow. At last he had hit the bull's-eye. He felt proud and happy. Then, glancing at the Alpine peaks turning rosy in the sunset light, he walked to the tree and pulled the arrow from it, calling, "Come, Rudi, let's go home. It's growing colder. I wish Father *would* come. He's so late. When he left home this morning, he told Mother he would be back before sunset with a chamois or a fox or something."

Prinz and the goats were far ahead. By the time the boys saw their log hut at the edge of a pine forest, the sun had already set. Only a faint glow still lingered on the crests of the mountains.

Rudi and Walter stopped on their way downward to kneel for a moment before a humble cross, built beside the path. Their father had taught them to do this. Then they chased each other down the well-worn path. When they reached home, the goats had already huddled

into a pen made of three large boulders. Here they felt safe from prowling bears and wolves, for in those far-off days of the thirteenth century many wild animals roamed the Alpine mountains.

Rudi darted into the hut as Walter grabbed a wooden bucket which hung on a peg and went to milk the goats. After his task was completed, he latched the gate which enclosed the pen, and carried the foaming milk bucket into the cabin. This was but one room with a big table in the middle. A candle glowed on this oak table, polished from years of use.

"The goats gave lots of milk tonight, Mother," said Walter gaily, as Hedwig, his fair-haired mother, took the bucket of milk. "We waited for Father until after the vesper bell rang, but he did not come. And I hit the target, Mother, right in the middle, the very last time I shot. I did, really I did, Mother. Rudi will tell you."

"But why shouldn't you, the elder son of William Tell, hit the bull's-eye?" Hedwig laughed as she leaned down and kissed her boy. Walter knew that she was teasing, yet her words pleased him. Still smiling, she poured milk into two carved wooden bowls and cut thick slices from a huge loaf of rye bread. Walter and Rudi soaked the bread in milk and ate it hungrily. They felt content in their little warm hut. Their mother loved them. Besides, was not their father the best bowman in the land of Uri?

"Father *is* late," said Walter as he drank the last drop of warm milk in his bowl.

"Yes, he is," sighed Hedwig, looking at the window. "As I was weaving this afternoon on the loom, I often thought I heard his step on the trail. But only a rock slipped on the mountainside or a tree groaned in the wind that rises from the valley at nightfall. In these days no woman knows if her man will return home when the sun drops behind the mountains."

Walter saw his mother's anxious face and said soothingly, "Don't worry, Mother, Father will come soon. He *always* comes home, and with game too, doesn't he?"

"You are very young, my son," answered Hedwig, softly. "You do not know all that goes on now in the land of Uri. It is not as it was when I was a child."

Rudi was already asleep, his head resting on the table beside his empty bowl. Hedwig lifted him gently and carried him to bed. She slipped off his buckskin pants and removed his linen blouse. Then she laid him down on the grass-filled mattress and covered him with a homespun blanket of goat's hair. As she drew the curtain about his bed, she spoke to Walter, who was sitting on a bench munching on a tart mountain apple. "He is just a baby," she said gently. "He is always so tired at night when he comes home, yet each morning when he awakens he is as fresh as a spring crocus."

"He tried to hold the crossbow all by himself today," added Walter, smiling, "but he is not yet strong enough. Sometimes I hold it for him and let him shoot. When he presses the trigger and the arrow goes 'twang' he feels so big and so happy."

"Just wait, Son, someday he will be a good bowman too, like your father," said Hedwig, taking up her knitting.

All was quiet in the hut as Walter gnawed on the apple. He heard the wind whining among the pine trees. A goat bleated contentedly. Prinz barked, hoping someone would let him in, but he was not allowed in the hut. His job was to watch the goats all night long.

"Mother," Walter asked at last, "why are you so sad tonight? What did you mean when you said times were better when you were a child? You warned me not to tell Rudi about the time Father and Grandfather were gone all night and did not come home until the next day. I overheard them talking, you remember. What did they do on that mountain-

top all night, Mother? Won't you tell me? I am eleven years old now."

Hedwig Tell let her knitting fall in her lap as she looked at her son sadly. "Yes, you are eleven years old, Walter, and soon will be a man. It *is* too bad you overheard your father and grandfather talking together. When your father gets excited, he talks too loudly. Sometimes I fear they may even hear him in the village! You know now that some men were plotting together and your father and grandfather were with them on the mountain. Since you do know this already, I must tell you more. It may be beyond your years, but you must try hard to understand, Son. Listen carefully."

Hedwig was so solemn that Walter whispered, "Yes, Mother, I will try hard to understand you." His eyes were big with wonder. His heart beat fast and he was not a bit sleepy.

"Years ago," began Hedwig very quietly," there was a king named Rudolph. He was ruler of Germany, Austria, and, of course, our canton of Uri. Also, our neighbor cantons of Schwyz and Underwalden. Each year he sent men to collect taxes from us, as rulers do. Otherwise he left us alone. Also, once a year he sent a nobleman to judge disputes among us: disputes over a cow, a goat, a boundary line or perhaps a forest. It seems there are always quarrels among people everywhere. As I said, a nobleman from Austria came yearly to judge us, and then returned to Austria again. But it is so different now."

"What do you mean, Mother, it is so different now? How is it different? Please tell me. I can understand. I am big."

Hedwig put her arms around him as she said, "The good king Rudolph died at last, as all men must. He was a good king as kings go. Then his son, Albrecht, became king. Albrecht was different from his father. He believed a king should rule with a hard hand, and that a king should hold a tight rein over his people. He did not want us to be as free as we had always been in the canton of Uri."

"Why, Mother?" asked Walter, wonder in his eyes.

"I will tell you, Son," continued Hedwig. "You know the big road, the Saint Gothard, that crawls up the Alps to the very top? That is the road to Italy."

"Yes," answered Walter, "I saw a pack train go through Altdorf one day, and the boys said the horses carried fine linens and such things from Lucerne and other cities. They said the men and horses were going to Italy."

"No doubt they were," replied his mother. "Everyone who travels over the Saint Gothard road must pay gold to Albrecht. The road goes right through Uri. And that is only one reason why the king wants our people to be tame. He gets much gold from the travelers over the road, big bags of gold. To be sure we are tame, Albrecht now sends bailiffs into the country and these bailiffs stay here all of the time. Some of them are low-born men like Gessler at Altdorf. He is not of noble blood, Walter, but a common man like ourselves. This Gessler is always about, prying into our affairs, we who have been free since there were mountains. Did you hear how Gessler put out the eyes of Arnold's old father when the bailiff could not find Arnold?"

"Yes, Grandfather told me about it," answered Walter, "I have hated Gessler ever since. He must be a coward to do that to an old man."

"Yes, he is a coward, Son," replied Hedwig. "He is building that great stone castle at Altdorf too, the castle of Zwing-Uri. Gessler makes the peasants work on the castle whether they wish to or not. Folks say that when the castle is finished, Gessler will live in it all of the time and watch us as a cat watches a mouse's hole, or the lion waits for the deer to graze before he springs. A part of the castle is a prison to put some independent mountain folk in when they even speak of freedom." Hedwig spoke so bitterly that Walter became fearful too. He often glanced at the curtained window, wondering if someone were outside listening.

"It has grown worse with each year," continued his mother. "At last your father and grandfather, with Arnold and Stauffacher, decided the time had come to act. It was useless to protest any more. These four men talked to friends they trusted. Several weeks ago, thirty-three men, eleven from each of the three cantons, met on the Rootli. Do you know where the Rootli is, Son?"

"Yes, Mother, I do," answered Walter softly, glancing at the window again, for he heard Prinz bark. "We passed below it once when I was fishing with father on the lake. Father said it was an open meadow surrounded by a dense forest."

"That is the Rootli," replied his mother, "a wild and lonely place, so far away from Altdorf that no soldier of Gessler's would know of it. Your father said that the thirty-three men argued all through the night. Not one of them wanted to shed blood, but all wanted to drive out the bailiffs. Toward morning they swore on a sword to stand together, come what may."

"They plan to revolt on the New Year," she went on. "If the people of one canton are attacked, the folk of the other two cantons promise to come and help them. All will fight as one nation. All will die together, too, if it ever comes to that. We are a stubborn race," said Hedwig.

"On the New Year we will revolt then?" asked Walter wonderingly.

"Yes," said Hedwig, determination in her voice, "and that will be soon. The year 1291 will dawn soon. Gessler's stone prison will *never* be finished, my son." Hedwig trembled as she spoke and Walter trembled, too, for he had never seen his mother so disturbed. She was usually so quiet and happy.

"So *that* is why I must not speak of the meeting on the Rootli," whispered Walter. "I understand now."

"Yes, that is the reason, Son. Do not whisper a word to anyone, even to Rudi or Marie, the herd girl. For if it should leak out that we will revolt on New Year's Day, your own father, Walter, might be the first one to die. Promise, Son, to keep this secret locked in your heart. Say nothing to anyone."

"On my crossbow I promise," said Walter solemnly. His heart beat fast and he was very excited. "Mother, when the people revolt on New Year's Day, will knights come up into the mountains on horses and will cannons go off and make a lot of noise? Will there be fires too?"

"There will be fires on the mountaintops, Son, signal fires," replied his mother, "but I hope there won't be real war. War means starvation and death, not only to soldiers, but to women and children too. War *always* means that." She sighed and rose, taking Walter by the hand. "Come, Son, to bed. Tomorrow dawns only too soon. Sometimes I grow afraid when your father does not come home at nightfall. I imagine him killed by one of Gessler's knights or soldiers. Or perhaps blinded, as was Arnold's old father, so that he cannot see his way home to us. These are women's fears, I guess, just women's fears. Sleep well, Son, may you not dream of evil things."

Hedwig kissed Walter and drew the curtain close about the bed. The boy lay for a long time, thinking over what his mother had told him. He heard her wash the wooden bowls. The fire crackled and spit. The wind moaned among the fir trees. Although he was tired, Walter could not go to sleep at once. He tossed and turned. He heard the church bells at Burglen toll the half-hour. Suddenly Prinz barked. Walter heard something heavy fall on the ground outside the hut. The great door squeaked on its rusty hinges.

Walter sat up in bed as he heard his father's deep voice. "Home at

last, Hedwig. I did not bring in the dead chamois I shot, knowing you for a good housekeeper. It is a fine, fat chamois, with a thick hide, Wife, but dirty and bloody."

Walter heard a bench squeak as his father sat upon it, and his mother laugh happily. Then came sounds of milk flowing into a bowl. Walter drew slowly aside the curtain just a little and peered out. In the candle-light he saw his father's weary face and his great beard. He heard his mother say soothingly, "Rest, Husband, I see you are worn. Refresh yourself. The boys are sound asleep. Walter thinks he is a great bowman for he hit the bull's-eye this afternoon. Rudi was so tired he fell asleep over his bowl of milk."

After a few moments of silence Walter heard his father say, "What a long day it has been. I shot the chamois as he leaped over the rocks on the edge of a glacier. The beast fell over a cliff as he died. I slipped and slid over the rocks for a long time to find him. I met your father too, Hedwig, as I came down the mountain. We talked long together. Do you know, Hedwig," he added, "the townsfolk say Gessler smells a rat. He notices that people carry their heads higher these days and so he is suspicious. How he would like to catch the leaders! He will try any new deviltry to find out who they are, too."

"You are much wrought-up, my husband," replied Hedwig soothingly. "Eat and drink now, and after that we will talk."

Walter lay down and listened to the wind moaning in the trees and the sound of the fire crackling on the hearth. Suddenly he heard his father speak again.

"Tomorrow morning, Hedwig, I must go to Altdorf."

"ALTDORF! Oh no, not to Altdorf, Husband. You will walk right into some clever trap that Gessler has laid for you." She spoke so shrilly that Walter sat up in bed.

He heard his father laugh and answer, "Trap, Wife, I'm too smart

for any trap Gessler could lay. I go to barter cheese for salt, perhaps, or to buy a new gown for the comeliest wife in all the mountains. I have a few skins to trade, too. Perhaps I may stop at the Baren Inn and drink with others there. I must go at dawn."

"But why do you go?" asked Hedwig, sorrowfully. "These are not reasons you have given me. They are not the *real* reasons. You jest with me."

Walter heard his father reply stubbornly, "I go because I *must* go, Hedwig. Your father says Gessler is looking for trouble. He is scheming. I must learn if any of our own men have betrayed us to him. If he knows about the revolt on the New Year."

"But, William, you know how quick your temper is, how sharp your tongue, how loud your voice especially when you get excited. Please don't go to Altdorf tomorrow," pleaded Hedwig.

"I will keep my tongue muzzled and my thoughts to myself, really I will, Hedwig. I will speak only with those I trust. Those I have known for years. A stone will be no more silent than I tomorrow," Walter heard his father promise.

"If I could only believe your words," sighed Hedwig. "You have never been as silent as a stone in all the years I have known you, Husband."

"I will be tomorrow, Wife. And if you still do not trust me, well then," and the mountaineer hesitated, "I will take Walter with me. A man does not take his elder son with him when he conspires, does he?"

Walter felt like jumping out of bed and rushing to his father, but he knew he must not. How wonderful it would be to go to Altdorf again! He would watch the blacksmith shoe a horse. He would play in the fountain with other village children. He might drink a glass of that sweet cider at the Baren Inn. Perhaps the bear would still be walking back and forth in his cage behind the inn and the old eagle drooping

on his perch. Altdorf was such a BIG place. Perhaps he might see a pack train march through the market place, going to Italy. He might even see a knight in shining armour riding a beautiful horse. *He might see Gessler, the tyrant, himself!*

"Well, if you *must* go," the boy heard his mother say at last, "perhaps you should take Walter. He may keep you from getting angry and talking too much." Then she added thoughtfully, "I told Walter tonight that he must not mention to anyone what he overheard when you and Father came home from the Rootli. He is only a child and you know how children forget and talk when they are full of a great secret. I do hope he remembers. It would be terrible if Gessler should hear of the revolt from a son of William Tell, wouldn't it?"

"Do not fear, Wife, Walter is a likely lad and an honest one," said William Tell. "I am sure he will hold his tongue. He is not like his old man, is he, Hedwig? A sieve full of holes?"

Walter heard his father laugh as he said this and his mother laugh, too. He turned over and lay close to Rudi for it was a cold night. He closed his eyes and just as he drifted off to sleep, he heard his mother murmur, "They sleep sweetly when they are young," and that was all Walter remembered.

2

Faith

"WAKE up, Son, and dress quickly. We are going to Altdorf together." William Tell's deep voice awakened Walter. He jumped from bed as he remembered his father's promise of the night before.

Soon father and son were tramping down the rough trail to Burglen. They passed through the tiny hamlet as William Tell nodded to right and left. Walter nodded too for he knew almost every child and dog of the village. Soon the two Tells were on the downward path again. The sun was just rising.

"When we get into Altdorf, Son," said the father, "keep by me until I say you may play with the children. I will visit the tanner's shop and trade for something for your mother. These skins on my back are worth something. She did not wish me to go to town today,

for she is fearful that I might talk too much or too loudly. You know the secret we must keep." Walter nodded. "We will keep it together, you and I," added Tell. He was in good spirits as he always was when he went to Altdorf.

Now they entered the ever-narrowing valley. It was fun to sing and shout and then listen to the sounds of their voices echo ever more faintly. Tell's strong dark legs moved along so fast that Walter could not sing much, he was so out of breath running. Then as the trail curved, Walter pointed to a cave in the hillside where lived a monk well-loved by the people of the land of Uri. He said, "Father, it must be lonely for Brother Klaus to live all by himself in that dark place and just pray all of the time."

"Perhaps it would be for you, Son," replied his father, "but Klaus seems happy. When any one of the mountain folk is ill or without bread, Klaus comes to comfort him. When a woman loses her husband or a mother her child, Klaus is there to pray with her. All men, Walter, do not like to do the same thing. Some like to hunt, others to fight, and still others to till the soil. Klaus is a man of God and I am sure he is happy even if he lives alone in that dark cave yonder."

Soon Walter saw the old roofs of Altdorf, and the stone towers of Zwing-Uri, Gessler's castle. Then Tell's happy mood changed. Walter heard him mutter, "That knave. As busy as a rat in a wheat rick. The towers grow higher each day. Soon Gessler will live there and spy upon all that we do. And put free men behind iron bars."

Walter said nothing. He was waiting eagerly to see the sign that hung from the roof of the Baren Inn. His father usually stopped at the inn. As they neared the place, Walter, to his surprise, saw his own grandfather, Walter Furst, standing before the inn as if he were really waiting for them. Walter loved his fun-making old grandfather, and ran to him, pulling on his cane.

"Well, well, bless my old eyes, what brings you two to Altdorf this cold day?" asked the older man. "It's going to rain, too. Why are you not herding the goats, Walter, and you, William, hunting for deer or fox?"

Tell winked, and in a low voice answered, "Perhaps the same thing that brings you here, Furst," which made Grandfather smile.

"Come in and let us drink together, then, and Walter too. He is growing up, that lad," said Grandfather Furst, looking down at the boy.

As the three entered the low door of the old inn, Tell stooped, for he was a big man. Walter followed and ran to the hearth to warm his cold hands. The men sought a dark corner of the room where they might talk and not be overheard. Soon a maidservant brought three brown mugs of cider on a tray. Walter joined his father and grandfather and slowly sipped the delicious drink. He was sorry when he could see the bottom of the mug and there was no more cider. The grownups were talking about things he did not understand and he twisted and fidgeted on the hard bench, hoping his father would buy another mug of cider for him. But his father just glanced down at him and said, "You are restless, Walter. Why don't you find the bear you are always talking about, and the eagle?" As he said this, he placed a forefinger over his mouth. Walter knew what he meant. He must keep the secret. Smiling, Walter ran through the room.

The bear was prancing up and down his cage in a never-ending trot, swinging his great head from side to side. He must hate that narrow cage, thought Walter. Village children were teasing the bear. They stuck branches of trees through the bars, hoping the wild animal might tear the branches with his wicked-looking claws, and thus frighten them. But the unhappy bear was used to children and paced his cage, thinking his own gloomy thoughts.

Then Walter watched a captured eagle in another cage. He was

perched on the dead branches of a tree. His eyes were shut and his tail feathers were falling out. He looked so sad and so old that Walter was sorry for him. For often, as he was herding in the mountains, the boy had watched great handsome eagles floating high in the heavens, carried ever upward by strong air currents. This old fellow must be dreaming of his mountaintops, thought Walter sadly.

The boy wandered around the building to the front door when suddenly he saw his father and grandfather step from the inn. His father looked very angry. Even his grandfather did not smile as Walter ran up to him.

"Come at once, Son. Let us go," was all that his father commanded. "Remember—quiet, and stay beside me."

"Yes," Walter answered, wondering at his father's change of mood. They passed through a narrow way between high houses and soon the village square or market place opened before them. Walter saw the familiar fountain in the center of the square but today two soldiers were beside it. One of them, an old fellow, was munching an apple. The other soldier was whittling on a stick with his dagger. They looked tired and bored. Then Walter noticed a long pole set in the ground beside the fountain. He had never seen that before. On the top of the pole fluttered a velvet hat with a feather in it, such a hat as Walter had often seen well-born people wear. He wondered why no children were playing in the fountain. No dogs lay in the dirt. No women came with water jars to draw water and to gossip together.

Suddenly a well-dressed villager passed by and nodded to the soldiers, doffing his cap and bending his knee to the hat on the pole. Walter felt his father's hand stiffen against his and heard him mutter, "Traitor." Nevertheless William Tell walked proudly on, looking neither to left or to right. Never did a man carry himself more nobly. His great bow hung from one massive shoulder. He walked with the dignity of a great

king. Past the fountain he strode, Walter clinging to him, past the soldiers, past the pole with the hat aloft, as if he did not see any one of them.

Suddenly Walter heard the younger soldier shout, "Stop, you! You dunce over there! Are you blind? See that hat on the pole, *you*. That's the hat of Austria, the ducal hat."

But father and son walked on unheeding. Soon the soldier munching the apple grabbed his spear and ran toward the mountaineer, yelling, "You knave, you blockhead. *Bow to that hat!* Or I'll run you through with this," and he lowered his great spear.

Only then did William Tell stop and eye the soldier fearlessly, as he shouted, "Hat, you dolt, what hat, I see no hat. I have business with the tanner." Tell's words made the soldiers very angry. One yelled, "Bend your knee to that hat, or we will crush your skull like a filbert, you and your filthy brat." The great mountaineer took one more step forward without replying, but the shouting of the soldiers had brought many townsfolk into the square. His way was blocked by soldiers with spears and by shouting people. Suddenly a guard blew on his bugle. Almost at once the market place was full of men, women, dogs, childr .
Other soldiers streamed in from narrow streets, to join the crowd, and Walter and his father were surrounded by a mob of people.

"Now for the last time, fool, bow before the ducal hat of Austria. Show you are a loyal subject of our governor, Gessler. Bow, you lout!" shouted a soldier.

The name of Gessler seemed to make Tell even more rebellious. He laughed in defiance, as Walter clung to him and shrank back from the lowered spears of the soldiers. "Go to the devil, you braggarts," he cried. "I am a man of peace. Why should I bow before a silly hat? A hat is not a lord. A hat is a thing of rags and feathers. It is nothing to bow down before."

The rugged mountaineer held his son's hand tightly and shouted these words so that all heard. The townsfolk milled around the soldiers in a dense crowd. Walter heard some of them curse the guards, call them "rats and knaves, dirt and dross."

Angry words flew like birds from people's mouths as they shouted at the soldiers. "Holy Mary," said one villager. "Poor wretch, he'll get it now," added another.

"Take your hands from me," commanded Tell as a guard seized him. "I have done no wrong. Take your hands from me, I say. I will not bow before that filthy hat. We've had enough of bowing and scraping in the land of Uri. Next thing you'll command us to bow before you, you bullies."

As they heard his insolent words, three angry soldiers grabbed the mountain man and pinned back his arms. "We dare you to insult the governor thus, you herder of goats."

A bugle sounded again, and the crowd scattered as mounted knights galloped into the market place. "Out of our way, you dumb brutes, out of our way," they commanded. Walter, almost in tears now, glanced up at them. And then he saw Gessler—the governor, Gessler. It could be no one else. The knight wore fine clothing, and rode a beautiful and spirited horse. But Walter thought he looked evil in spite of his grandeur.

"What goes on here?" demanded Gessler. The crowd was now deathly quiet. "Oh, so it is you, William Tell, the man of the mountains," jeered Gessler, seeing his soldiers hold the bowman by the arms. "In trouble again, I see. For what do my men now hold you so tightly, you herder of goats?"

The mountaineer did not reply. Then a soldier spoke. "He will not bow before the ducal hat, my Lord."

"Oh, so he is too fine to bow before the hat of Albrecht of Austria, is he? Tell, the windbag. Bow, I say, before your betters or we will run you through," warned Gessler.

Tell was silent. He did not move. He looked at Gessler and his eyes were like black coals, burning with hatred. Walter trembled but he held himself proudly like his father.

"So you have no tongue in that filthy mouth now. Who are your friends, Tell? There must be more like you in your mountains. Speak or you will be sorry."

Now the great bowman was really angry. He bellowed like a mad bull. The people could hear every word he said. "I will not bend my knee before a hat. I will bow only to those more truly noble than I. Men of gentle birth. Wise men. The man of God and the good Lord himself. I am a man of peace. I will not bend my knee before a hat of rags and feathers. A hat is nothing to worship. A well-born man, a noble, is something else."

How angry Gessler became at these words. He knew that Tell was jeering at his common birth. Tell was shouting his meanness to the whole village of Altdorf. Tell was insulting him.

"Oh, so you are too fine to bow before your betters," snarled Gessler, white with fury. Then a sly look came into his face as he glanced sharply down at Walter, clinging to his father and hiding his face.

"Who is that brat that clings so cravenly to you, Tell?" asked Gessler.

"My son, Walter, my elder son," replied Tell, looking at Walter and pressing his hand.

"Is that your only son, braggart?" asked Gessler.

"No, I have another son, Rudolph by name."

"I see you have your crossbow with you, Tell. I have heard it said you are a good bowman, the best in the canton of Uri. Is that true?"

"I know not if it is true," answered Tell, modestly, "for there are many good bowmen in Uri. But some folk have said so."

A townsman shouted, "Tell is the best of us all."

"Let us see then, how good a bowman you really are, lout. Take that

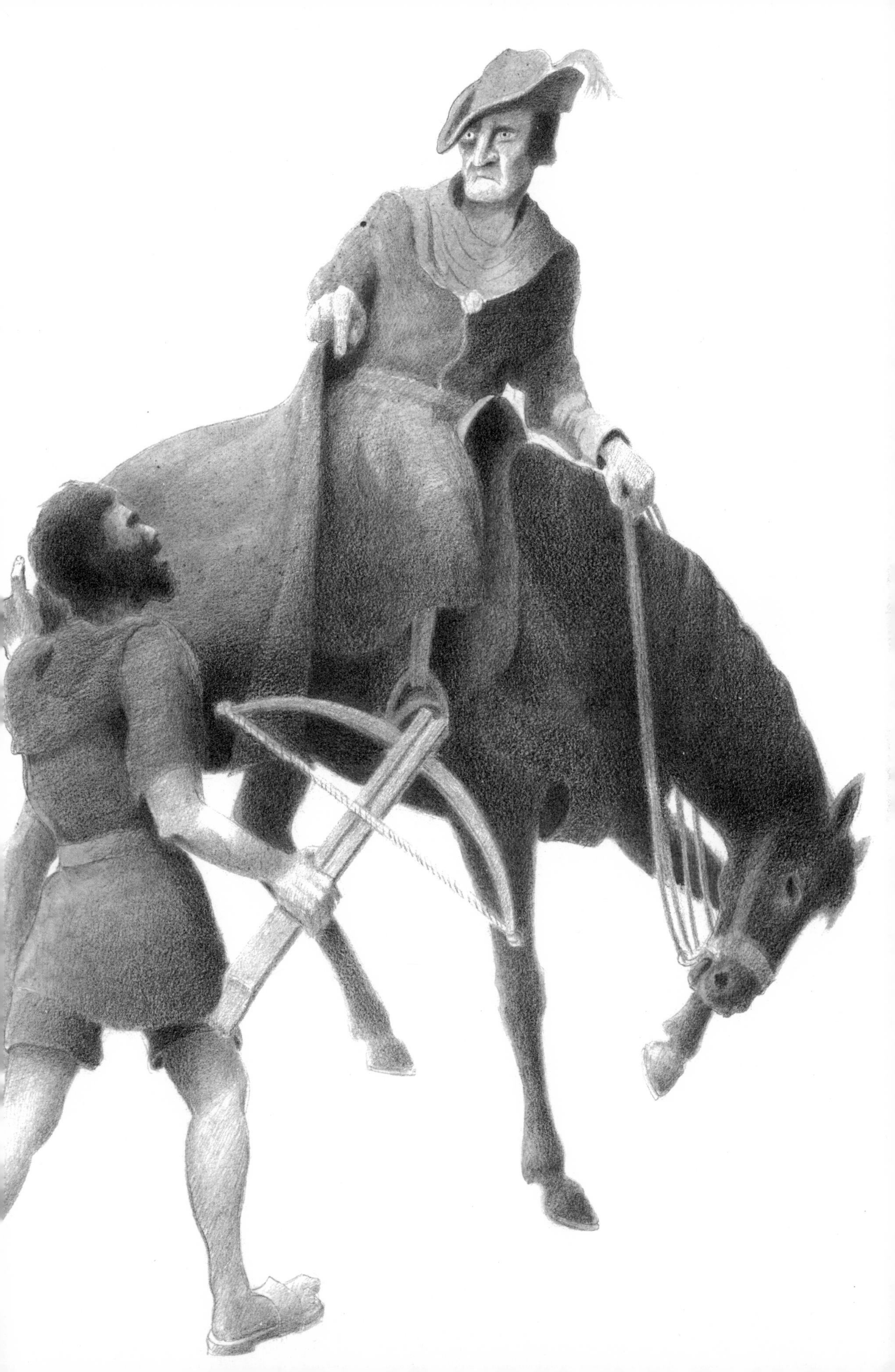

cowardly boy, men, and place him against yon linden tree. Put an apple on his head. Tell, if you can shoot the apple from your son's head, you shall go free. But . . . if any harm comes to the boy or you miss the apple, you will *both* die," shouted the governor.

A gasp of horror floated through the crowd as Walter heard people cry, "The wretch . . . knave . . . " But Gessler only smiled an evil smile as he pointed to the linden tree.

At last Tell found his voice. "You cannot ask this of me, Governor," he pleaded. "This is an innocent lad, and my first-born. He has done no harm to anyone."

"But I thought you were such a great bowman, Tell," retorted the governor. "I see you are just a bag of wind with the face of a lion and the heart of a deer."

At these stinging words, Walter shouted in his high boyish voice so that all heard, "Father, I am not afraid. I will stand at the linden tree and they need not bind me. I will stand as still as a rock. You will hit the apple, Father. You always hit the chamois right in the heart. Shoot, Father, I am not afraid."

"See the boy, Gessler, how he believes in his father!" shouted a woman shrilly. The soldiers seized Walter and bound him to the linden tree, while mothers clutched their children to them fiercely, as if to shield them from the evil bailiff. Walter stood silently as a guard placed a large apple upon his head. He could see the townsfolk brandishing sticks and threatening the knights. A boy threw a stone and a horse reared.

Gessler commanded, "Quiet, you people of Altdorf. Quiet." Then looking down at Tell he said, "This is your chance, fool, to show how skilled you are with the bow."

The soldiers freed the mountaineer. He slipped his bow from his shoulder and raised it. He placed the arrow. Then standing quietly he gazed at his son tied to the linden tree.

Suddenly a monk, his head lowered, walked slowly toward Gessler. As he reached the governor, he raised his head. "Governor," he pleaded, "This is a simple man of the mountains. He knows not what he does. He means no harm. He loves his son, as all good men love their sons. Do not, I pray you, put him to this test of skill. Take council with your knights. Tell is not a dastardly fellow, only an unlettered one. By the Holy Mary, do not do this cruel thing."

But Gessler only scowled at the monk and replied, "Father, I must do this. I must prick this windbag. The people *must* obey their earthly masters as they do their heavenly master."

The holy man withdrew in silence, fingering his rosary and praying. William Tell knelt on the ground. He raised his heavy crossbow again to his shoulder and took careful aim. Not a sound was heard. Even the dogs stopped barking: the horses prancing. The mountaineer was about to press the trigger of his crossbow, when the sight of his slender son, standing so quietly at the linden tree, overcame him. He put down his bow and groaning aloud, he pleaded, "My lord, have pity. Spare my son. I cannot do this to an innocent, trusting child. I cannot. I cannot. Have pity on us, my lord."

"Ho, ho, so it is 'my lord' at last, Tell. So you cannot. The strong mountain man cannot. He trembles like the leaves of that linden tree yonder. See how pale he is! What a rare sight! Tell, the great windbag, is trembling like a frightened woman. Where is your boasted skill with the bow, Tell?"

As Walter heard these bitter words, he shouted above the din, "Shoot, Father, shoot. I am not afraid. God is watching over us."

Walter's voice seemed to bring back his father's courage. He took another arrow from his quiver and slipped it into his girdle. Then he quickly raised the heavy crossbow to his shoulder as muscles rippled on his brown arms. He sighted the apple on his son's head. He pulled back the drawstring. Many of the townsfolk were now on their knees praying. Gessler eyed every move that Tell made. Then, with a grim smile and almost without warning, the great bowman quickly and surely squeezed the trigger of his faithful bow. The arrow sped like a ray of light. Walter suddenly felt the apple on his head split, tremble and then fall to the ground. The nose of the arrow buried itself in the old gnarled trunk of the ancient linden tree.

A great sigh of relief, like a sudden wind, passed over the heads of the people. Then all at once sounds of jubilation burst forth as the people saw that Walter was safe from harm. "The mighty Tell, Tell the hero," the people shouted, surging toward the bowman as he stood there, his dark body glistening with sweat, proud and erect. The people tried to reach him to carry him on their shoulders like the hero he was, but soldiers barred their way. Women cried, others prayed, while still others shouted. Their happiness made Gessler even more angry.

When guards unbound Walter, he picked up the two halves of the apple and ran toward his father, crying, "See, father, you cut the apple in two pieces."

A soldier blew on a horn to quiet the happy crowd and in the silence Walter heard Gessler shout, "You *did* hit the apple, Tell, and not your son. You *are* a bowman as men say. But what of that second arrow you thrust so quickly into your girdle?"

William Tell, feeling suddenly weak and tired, just looked at the governor and said, "That is the custom of bowmen, Governor."

"Answer me, Tell, I want the truth. Why was the second arrow hidden in your girdle? Tell me and I will spare your life."

William Tell was a simple, trustful man of the mountains. He believed Gessler's words, for the word of a knight was supposed to be truth itself. So he replied honestly, "Had I killed my son, Governor, this arrow would have found your heart."

CONRAD

Gessler suddenly flushed with anger. "Oh, so *that* is the truth, at last," he growled. "I promised to let you live, and that I will do on my word as a knight. But I will put you where you will never again see the sun rise in the mountains nor the moon set behind the peaks. Drag this man to the boat on the lake, soldiers. We will take him to the dungeon of the Castle of Kussnacht."

Walter was pushed from his father's side as the angry people of Altdorf followed the soldiers dragging Tell away. The boy was knocked down in the dense crowd and lay in the dirt, crying. Then at last the shouting and the noise faded away as Walter got slowly to his feet. Through his tears he saw the market place was now completely empty. The pole and the ducal hat lay on the ground. Then Walter saw Grandfather Furst hastening toward him. The old man clasped the crying boy to him and said soothingly, "Don't cry, Walter, we will go home. Mother is waiting for you."

"But, Grandfather," gulped Walter when he could talk once more, "what will they do with Father? Are they going to kill him now after he hit the apple? Gessler promised not to. Will they put him in prison?"

"Quiet, lad," soothed grandfather. "Your father is a brave man. They will not dare to kill him now. The people would revolt. Instead they may keep him a while in prison. But never fear, you will see him again soon."

Walter and his grandfather half ran and half walked up, up, up the mountain trail toward home. Great dark clouds gathered overhead. Soon the rain fell in torrents. They reached home at last, wet and shivering. When Walter saw his mother, he ran and buried his face in her skirts like a small boy, for he was frightened and very, very tired. Hedwig put him to bed and while Grandfather Furst told her the story of the sad day, he sobbed himself to sleep.

3

Waiting

RAIN poured down upon the land of Uri all that night. The angry winds knocked down a tall pine tree near the hut, just missing it. Boulders slid down the mountainside as smaller rocks rolled about on the roof of the hut. A mountain stream just beyond the goat pen overflowed its banks. When dawn came, the Tell home was damp and cold as rain had leaked through holes in the roof and had dripped down the chimney. The wood in the fireplace was wet and would not burn. It was almost as cold within the house as without. Nevertheless Grandfather Furst, who had stayed all night, was up early to milk the goats, so that Walter and Rudi could stay in bed where it was warm.

Soon after breakfast a few neighbors began to come. Others followed, and before long Walter and Rudi wondered if *all* the people of Burglen

were trying to crowd into the single smoky room. More came constantly. They had heard rumors of the shooting at Altdorf and like all country people were curious to know more. They especially wanted to know what had happened to William Tell, now their hero.

A neighbor brought Hedwig a hindquarter of venison. Another, a flagon of sweet cider. Then little Marie, a playmate of the Tell boys who also herded goats on the mountainside, handed Walter a pair of woolen socks. She had knit them herself during the long hours of herding. "They'll keep you warm, Walter," she said, "now that it is wintertime. My, you must have been scared yesterday when the soldiers bound you and you had to stand and be shot at," she whispered to him.

"No, I wasn't scared a bit," replied Walter. "I knew all the time that Father couldn't miss."

Rudi only peered at the crowd of people from behind the bed curtain. He was still a little boy and shy of strangers. As each neighbor entered the hut, Grandfather began again the story of the exciting morning in Altdorf. Walter noticed how red in the face his grandfather got during each account and how excited he grew as the day went on. There never seemed an end of the people coming and going. It was like a great church festival or a wedding.

But the hours passed and the rain finally stopped. The boys ran to look after the goats, glad to be out of doors, and away from the hut so full of smoke and neighbors. Just then Walter noticed Ulrich, the baker's son, puffing up the hill. When he reached the door Walter asked him, "Have you learned anything about my father?" But the boy did not answer and rushed into the cabin, full of importance. Walter and Rudi followed on his heels.

"You must have more news," Walter heard his grandfather exclaim to Ulrich.

"I have," grasped the boy breathlessly, for he was tired from running.

"Out with it lad, out with it. Don't stand there like a dumb ox."

Grandfather was irritated by the boy's slowness. Ulrich only walked over to the smoking fireplace and warmed his hands as if he had no news at all. Then he said, "Wolfgang, the fisherman, on the Lake of the Forest Cantons, saw it himself."

"Saw what, Ulrich?" questioned Hedwig, eagerly, taking the boy by the shoulders.

"He told Rudenz, the herdsman, and Rudenz ran all the way up to Burglen to bring my father the news," replied Ulrich.

"What news, silly?" asked an old crone, peevishly.

The people all waited breathlessly while the baker's son enjoyed keeping them waiting. "Well," drawled Ulrich, at last, "Wolfgang was pulling in his nets yesterday when the storm broke. He saw a large boat tossing about on the lake. The waves were high. At first Wolfgang could not see who was in the boat because it was pitching very much. But as it whirled nearer, he saw there were soldiers in the boat, and then . . . " Ulrich hesitated and waited for all eyes to be centered on him. "And then . . . he saw William Tell was steering."

"William Tell steering the governor's boat . . . impossible!" exclaimed the people as in one voice. Walter shoved his way through the packed crowd until he stood just beside the baker's son.

"No, he was not mistaken," Ulrich continued. "He knows Tell. Tell *was* at the tiller. Gessler was there too and he was holding his belly, for he was seasick. Rudenz could make nothing of this strange sight. He did not know what had happened in Altdorf at all. And as he watched . . . " Here Ulrich lowered his voice and the people crowded closer to him. "As he watched," he repeated, "Tell steered the boat toward a rocky ledge below Axenstein. Just as the prow touched the rock, Tell jumped, and then, quick as a flash of lightning, he kicked the boat back into the water and ran into the shelter of the forest like a doe."

A great shout filled the cabin. "That Tell, oh that Tell. Praise be

to the Blessed Virgin." Women wept and Hedwig fell to her knees and bowed her head.

"Did the soldiers shoot at him?" asked Grandfather.

"No, Wolfgang says no," replied the boy, delighted at the excitement he had caused. "They were too surprised and too seasick. The soldiers were pea-green with sickness. The boat tossed about like a mad thing. Wolfgang could not see much of them for the rain, but he *thinks*," and here the boy waited for his audience to look at him, "he *thinks* the boat sank and all in it were drowned!"

"Drowned—the governor drowned!" exclaimed the people in joy. "May Gessler and his knaves lie tonight in the deep waters of the lake. May God have pity on their black souls," said Grandfather crossing himself.

"If it were only true," sighed Hedwig, "if it were only true." As she said this, she put her arms about Walter and Rudi and they sat together on a bench by the fire. Walter stared into the embers. It seemed he could see in them a rocking boat full of men. Then his father jumped from it to shore and kicked the boat back into the water. Where was his father now, he wondered, looking up from the fire. Was he hiding in the cold, wet forest? Was he sitting in some friendly woodcutter's hut, warm and secure? If he only knew!

"Tell is like a cat," said one of the neighbors. "He will find his way home," said another quietly to Hedwig, patting her on the shoulder, for Tell's wife was weeping again.

In a moment Walter heard her whisper something to Grandfather, for he raised his hand and said, "Hush all. Friends, we know you have come to comfort us, but Hedwig is weary and would be alone. I ask of you to leave us in peace. We will send Walter and Rudi to the village if we learn anything new."

Walter nodded. The people understood, for they walked out quietly and at last the hut was empty of all but the Tell family.

"Mark my word, Daughter," said Grandfather sighing and sitting wearily on a bench, "every woman's son will be coming here now with a new rumor until at last we learn the true story. Each man adds a little to what he has heard, and the story grows like a snowball. We can but wait and pray."

"Let us eat now, the boys are hungry," said Hedwig as she brought a big bowl of whey left after making goat's cheese. They all pulled up to the table and as they were eating, Prinz barked. Someone knocked timidly on the door.

"Come in, friend," said Grandfather wearily, thinking it was just another curious neighbor. The door opened slowly. There stood Klaus, the hermit, the man of God, in his long dark robe. Klaus had heard of Tell's escape from a passer-by and had come to comfort the herdsman's family.

"I learned of your sorrow, Hedwig," he said quietly, "and would pray with you for your husband's return. He is indeed a brave man, and you have a brave son, too," he added putting his hand on Walter's head. Together they all knelt on the floor as Brother Klaus prayed, "May the good Lord who watches over the weak, the pure, the innocent now watch over brave William Tell. Bring him home safely and keep him from all harm. Amen."

Afterwards Brother Klaus shuffled from the hut quietly and disappeared in the darkness. When Walter closed the door after the holy man, his heart too was comforted. Soon they all went to bed. Hedwig let Prinz sleep inside by the fire this one night. She was the last one of the family to close her sad eyes. The fire flickered on the hearth and the wind whistled among the pine trees. A goat bleated sadly now and then. Water dripped down the chimney as regularly as the ticking of a clock. The church bells tolled and tolled the passing of the hours, while the family of William Tell slept restlessly.

Just as dawn was breaking, Walter Tell awakened, for Prinz was jumping against the door and whining. Walter heard footsteps. A grayish light came through the single window. And then all at once the door burst open, and in the dim light of the new day, Walter saw his father. He stood in the doorway trembling, his tunic torn, and streaks of dried blood running down his arms like dark rivers. He was drooping with weariness, and covered with mud and dirt.

"My husband, oh my husband!" cried Hedwig, jumping from her bed. She ran and clasped Tell around the neck and sobbed on his breast. "You have come at last, at last. How anxious we have been. Oh, my husband!"

Grandfather had awakened too and was staring sleepily at Tell.

"I am spent," sighed Tell at last. "Let me sit. I have walked through the night and have not slept, so it seems, for years."

"Yes, yes, take off those muddy clothes, my husband. I will bring you dry ones," uttered Hedwig, tears of joy in her eyes, as Walter and Rudi, now fully awake, danced about their father.

"Father, Father, how did you get away?" they cried. "Did the boat really sink, Father? Tell us, tell us, how did you get away?"

"Children, children, be quiet," said Hedwig to them sharply. "Don't you see your father is sick and must eat and rest and be quiet? Later he will tell you."

The boys stared at their father with anxious eyes. He looked wounded. His face was drawn and haggard like that of an old man.

William Tell put on dry clothing, washed the blood from his arms, and the mud from his face and neck. Then he sat down and ate and drank until he could eat and drink no more. After his meal he seemed to grow younger with the minutes. Soon he lifted Rudi on his lap, while Walter stood beside him, his hand upon his father's shoulder. All were waiting.

4

Courage

TELL began, "Gessler's soldiers bound me with iron chains. I fought with all my strength and it took five of the rascals to hold me. They dragged me along. The people of Altdorf ran cursing after them, throwing stones. A horse reared and struck a little maid. Gessler and his knights rode ahead of us and did not look back. How I hated that tyrant! If I had been free, I would have cut his heart to ribbons with an arrow."

"You would, Father, you would too," echoed Walter proudly.

"What happened then, Father?" asked Rudi, tugging at his father's beard.

"Be quiet, Rudi, and stop pulling at my beard or I'll put you down," scolded Tell.

"Rudi, Rudi, be good," said Hedwig soothingly.

William Tell continued, "When we reached the lake, the guards threw me into the bottom of a large boat tied at the water's edge. The sky was very dark and it was raining across the lake. The wind blew, too, and there were whitecaps on the water. Those white-livered soldiers were fearful when they saw high waves. They knew about the Lake of the Forest Cantons and how dangerous it could be in time of storm."

"Were they all foreigners, the soldiers, I mean?" asked Walter.

"Yes, most of them were," answered his father, "but one, Peter by name. He was a good and kind man. When he saw that the chains were cutting my arms, he loosened them a bit. Peter once lived in Burglen as a lad. Do you remember him, Hedwig, Peter, the tanner's son?"

"Oh yes, Peter," mused Hedwig, "of course I remember him well. When I was young I used to play with him in the village fountain. I did not know he had become a soldier for the governor. I would have thought better of Peter. He was such a sweet lad."

"Men do many things, Hedwig, that they do not wish to, just to live," answered Tell sharply. "Don't blame Peter. He was poor and had no trade. Men like Peter become common soldiers. You remember how many of our lads go abroad when they are grown and hire out to kings and dukes all over Europe."

"Of course," sighed Hedwig, putting her arms protectively about Walter as if he too might some day become a soldier. "But Peter was such a sweet lad, just like Walter and Rudi are now."

Walter felt uneasy. He thought it might be nice to become a soldier some day when he grew up and wear a helmet and carry a long spear. Yet he knew his mother would never want him to.

Tell continued, "I saw that the soldiers feared the lake. It is a long way to Kussnacht by boat. They whined that the lake was dangerous in storm. There were many hidden rocks, men said, where boats had sunk. But stubborn Gessler commanded, 'Enter the boats, men, and let us be off!'

"The Austrians took their places at the oars and one handled the tiller. When we started out, a stroke of lightning flashed on the mountaintop above the Rootli. A sign—I thought—a sign. None of those stupid foreigners knew a thing about the Lake of the Forest Cantons. It takes years to know the whims of the lake. Peter knew these whims and he was pale, not from sickness, but from fear."

"Once, Father, I was fishing on the lake and a storm came up and I saw whitecaps just as you say. We brought our boat to shore at once," Walter exclaimed.

"Let Father go on with the story, Walter, and don't interrupt," Hedwig scolded.

"The boat skipped about on the water like a cork," continued William Tell. "No one could stand. Had I been free of the chains, I could have managed it but those numskulls thought they knew it all. How the wind blew! The waves were higher than this hut, my sons, much, much higher. The rain made a gray blanket about us so we could not see. I lay at the bottom of the boat soaked with water. I was shivering as with ague. The soldiers grew pale. They retched and belched. The good cider and deerflesh they had eaten at the Inn at Altdorf that morning spilled from them into the water.

"Peter knew we might sink at any moment. He stared at Gessler and then I heard him plead, 'My Lord, there is a man in this boat, the prisoner, who knows the Lake of the Forest Cantons as if he had drawn every rock and current on parchment. Please have pity and save us all. For the Virgin's sake, let William Tell take the tiller. He alone can guide us to safety. He has known this lake and its moods since he was a lad.'

"Gessler looked startled. He stared down at me in the bottom of the boat, wet, shivering and bleeding. Peter pleaded again. Several of the Austrians, afraid for their lives, pleaded with him too. Gessler was sick

himself. He belched and retched and was the color of mustard. Suddenly after a fit of dizziness, he commanded, 'Unbind the prisoner. Steer the boat, Tell, and steer it to safety or your life is forfeit.' "

"Ha, ha," laughed Grandfather, "what chance had the tyrant to do anything about your life if he himself lay at the bottom of the lake?"

"Yes, that was the joke of it," laughed Tell, "but no one saw a joke just then. They were all too sick and frightened. They unbound me quickly. I grabbed the tiller. The waves were now mountain-high and the wind blew us this way and that way. But in just a little while I had that boat under control and it was pitching in the direction I wished it to go. For I had a plan and the plan did not include Gessler and his milksop crew."

"What was the plan, Father?" inquired Walter breathlessly.

"Now if you will only wait, Walter, your father will tell you," said his grandfather. "Go on, William."

"As we drew into quieter waters near shore, I steered the boat toward that flat rock below Axenstein," continued the mountaineer. "I heard Gessler say happily, 'We will soon land, men. Then we will rest in the forest until the storm is over. Toward evening we will row to Kussnacht.'

"I smiled to myself. They would never rest in that forest. In a moment the prow of the boat struck solid rock and I jumped ashore. When I felt the rock under my feet, I kicked the boat with all my strength. It whirled around and a crazy current caught it. In no time at all it was far out in the lake. As I ran for the shelter of the forest, I heard the soldiers cursing me. They would have shot at me, but the boat was rocking too much. I yelled, 'We'll meet again, Gessler!' Then I hid behind a tree. I was sorry that I could not take Peter with me."

"Yes, Peter was such a sweet lad," murmured Hedwig.

"Father, didn't any of the soldiers shoot at you?" asked Rudi.

"Rudi, Father just said they didn't," quieted his mother. "They were too sick. Don't ask any more silly questions."

"What then, Father?" asked Walter.

"Well, boys, you should have seen that boat! As I peered from behind a tree in the forest, what a rare sight I saw! Gessler was leaning over the side of the boat. He was very sick. The wind had blown his elegant hat from his head. It swirled around in the water and then it sank. But I could not afford to gloat over his misery any longer—I had much to do and quickly. I sat down on a log for a few moments, thinking. Perhaps the currents and the winds between them might sink Gessler and his soldiers. But I could not be *sure*. If they should escape drowning, I would be a hunted man forever. A price would be posted in every village for my capture. I could never live in my own home again."

"Really, Father, couldn't you sleep in your own bed as you always do?" asked Rudi.

"No, little Rudi, I would have to sleep in the forest with a rock for a pillow.

"And if Gessler could not find me, he might pour his wrath upon you, my dear Hedwig, or on you, my Father, or on my two sons. You remember how he blinded Arnold's old father when he could not catch Arnold?" said William Tell.

"That is true," nodded Grandfather.

"And so," continued Tell, "I made up my mind. I would waylay Gessler. If the boat should finally weather the storm, he and his knights would very likely land near the road that leads to the Castle of Kussnacht. I would wait for him as he rode along the 'Hollow Way' as it is called, to his castle. It was damp and cold in the forest. I walked all afternoon and all that night without food or rest. Toward dawn I came to the hut of Nicholas, your old friend, Father."

"Yes, Nicholas, the woodcutter, a good man," answered Grandfather smiling.

"He was good to me," replied Tell. "He gave me bread and meat. He warmed me at his fire. After a few hours I started out again. I walked and walked. My legs were scratched in the dense thickets. See," and Tell pointed to his legs.

"Oh, Father, you *are* scratched up," said Rudi and Walter, touching their father's scarred legs gently.

"I didn't notice the scratches very much," continued Tell, "I was so anxious to reach the Hollow Way. I saw bear and deer and fox too, but did not stop for I had much bigger game than they in mind. When I finally reached the sunken road, I was cold and very hungry but did not dare to make a fire. I hid in the gaping hole of a huge pine tree away from the wind and waited and waited. I waited long. Many times I thought I heard sounds of horsemen, but they were sounds of nature: the wind, rocks slipping, frogs croaking. I must have slept, for suddenly I awoke as I heard a new sound, a horse neighing. I listened. The sound came faintly again. It seemed nearer. Then I heard a dog bark and a horse's hoof strike a rock far-off."

"My, Father, you must have been scared then," chimed in little Rudi.

"No, Son, I was too anxious to be scared. I got my bow ready and I waited. The mother doe was not more silent than I was. Soon came more sounds: a shout—a horse's neigh—pounding of hoofs. I was sure now and I was ready. I peered from behind a tree, and at last I saw something moving. Men on horseback. It might be another party of horsemen I thought. Perhaps not Gessler at all. I must wait and be sure before I struck. It was hard enough for me to kill Gessler in cold blood, even after what he had done to me, but I must not kill the wrong man."

"How long did you wait, Father?" sighed Walter, his eyes big with suspense.

"Not long I guess, Son, not long. Soon I saw horses and riders. As they came nearer and nearer they would suddenly disappear, for the road wound around big rocks and trees. But soon I could not doubt. The first horse approached me and I saw the knight riding; it was indeed Gessler. But how the bluster had gone from him! He rode wearily, a tired man. I had the arrow in place, the thong tight. My fingers were on the trigger as I waited. I had waited so long for this moment to come that I was a little nervous. I must get Gessler with the first arrow! I could not gamble on a second one. My fingers quivered as the horseman came nearer and nearer. He suspected nothing. Then the road curved. Between two great rocks rode Gessler toward me. Now he faced me. I whispered to my bow, 'bow be strong, arrow be swift!' "

"Oh, Father!" exclaimed the two boys.

"Yes, the arrow was swift, my sons. Gessler never knew what hit him. He slumped to the ground like a sack of meal as his horse reared. His terrified soldiers stopped and dismounted quickly. They rushed to the aid of their dead lord. It was too late. But I had no time to watch their terror. I ran back through the forest and by nightfall I reached the hut of Kunz."

"So the governor is really dead," sighed Hedwig.

"Yes, Gessler is dead. He died as any man dies, poor or rich, great or lowly. He is as dead as that log yonder," said Tell, looking into the smouldering fire.

"Kunz was happy when I told him of Gessler's end," continued Tell. "He slapped his thighs and bellowed. His daughter had suffered at the hands of one of Gessler's soldiers, so you know how he felt. He brought forth a bottle of rare old wine and we drank to the freedom of Uri."

"And of Schwyz and Underwalden, too," added Grandfather.

"Yes, to the freedom of us all," replied Hedwig.

"Alight with wine and food, I hastened homeward," said Tell. "I did not feel tired. Perhaps I was wrought up over what had happened. I walked and walked. No man saw me but Kunz. I told no man of

Gessler's death. I slipped through Altdorf and Burglen like a shadow and not even a dog barked."

Walter and Rudi sighed. The story was over. They looked up into their father's face and their eyes were shining. "But, Father," asked Walter, "won't the soldiers look for you now? Will you have to hide in the forest in the daytime and sleep among the rocks at night as Arnold did?"

"No, Son, I do not have to hide now," replied Tell, stroking Hedwig's hand, for she was trembling. "Now that the governor is dead, those weak-kneed soldiers of his have no one to command them. They will hide from us like rats in a hayrick. They may even run away to Austria in the dark of the night. They love their own skins too much to venture into our mountains to search for me. We mountain folk can shoot."

"Still no one can be *too* sure," sighed Hedwig, still fearful. "It is true no man saw you shoot Gessler, but Kunz knows it. He may tell others for he is happy. The story may be all over Uri soon."

"Well, what if it is?" answered Tell proudly. "Remember Uri is big and it takes time to get a story all over Uri. And the New Year comes soon."

"It is as you say, Hedwig," added Grandfather. "The soldiers may guess who killed the governor, but the New Year comes soon now and we will revolt. We will revolt together."

Walter glowed at the thought of the New Year and the revolution.

"Already the herdsmen in the mountains are gathering wood," continued Grandfather. "You should see the huge pile on Hockalp, boys. In a few days the people of Uri will drive the rascals out."

"But, Father, what will the king do when he learns that Gessler is dead?" asked Walter, worried about his father.

"Do? It will take a long time before the news reaches him, Son. Austria is very far away. When Albrecht hears about Gessler's death, he may be too busy with other people and their revolts against him. No one likes Albrecht. And by that time we will be free."

Walter was silent as he thought, If only Mother would let Rudi and me go to Hockalp on New Year's morn. Wouldn't it be wonderful to see the huge fires blaze on the mountaintop and to watch the great peaks lit up by all of the signal fires!

He turned to his mother and said, "Mother, Rudi and I are going out." She hardly heard him she was so thoughtful. When the boys were outside, Walter whispered to Rudi, "Rudi, let's go up to Hockalp and see if there really is a pile of logs there as Grandfather just said." They ran breathlessly up the mountain trail.

5

The Dawn

"WHAT a good lad you have been today, Walter," said Hedwig Tell. "You have kept the water pail full of water. You have carried in wood and the fire has always been blazing." Hedwig Tell was weaving linen on the loom. She continued, "And not once today, Son, have I heard you quarreling with Rudi. You are both growing up."

Her words of praise made Walter a little uncomfortable. He *had* tried to be helpful all day, but yet he had a special reason for doing so. He wanted to go to Hockalp that night. This was the last day of the year 1290. With the dawn of the new year perhaps three brave little cantons would free themselves of Austrian tyranny. He wanted to be there.

Walter leaned on the loom and watched the shuttle dart back and forth. Then he said, "Mother, ever since Father and Grandfather left yesterday for the town, Rudi and I have been playing we were grown-up men and tried to take their places."

"Oh so *that* is it!" smiled his mother. She leaned over and felt playfully of Walter's shoulder blade. "What! Do I feel angels' wings sprouting from your shoulders, my son?"

Walter grinned. He loved his mother to joke with him. Then she began to weave again. The shuttle made a homely rhythm that Walter loved as it flew across the warp. After a long silence, the boy said, "Mother, please stop weaving for a moment. I want to ask you something." His eyes were shining and he was eager and anxious. His mother laid down the shuttle and waited for him to speak. Rudi was playing on the floor with a toy cow his father had carved for him. Suddenly Walter burst out, "Mother I'm eleven years old and soon will be twelve. You know what's happening tonight on Hockalp. The signal fires . . . Mother can't I go up on Hockalp at midnight? Please, please, Mother!"

Rudi bounded up from the floor and asked eagerly, "Can't I go along, Mother, can't I go with Walter?" Rudi had the keenest ears for things he was not supposed to hear.

"You'll freeze up there, Rudi. It's cold at midnight, you know," warned his brother.

"Oh I'll not freeze a bit. I'll put on that bear coat that's so warm and my fur mittens. I'll not freeze, will I, Mother?"

"Quiet children, don't tease," she scolded. She laid her shuttle down and gazed through the window, as if she were looking at something far, far away. The boys stared at her silently. After a long pause she said, "Yes, you may both of you go. But if I let you go, Walter, you must take good care of Rudi. Don't let him get lost or chilled. Will you?"

"No, I won't, Mother, I promise. Marie will be there, too, and we will both take care of Rudi, if you'll only let me go."

"Yes, Son, you may go. There may never again in your lifetime be another night like this one in the land of Uri. It will be a night I want you to remember when you are old. I want you to know while you are young, my son, that brave men will risk all they have for a belief. Now let us eat, and when it grows late, put on your bearskin capes and woolen socks. It will be bitterly cold at midnight on Hockalp."

Several hours later the Tell boys climbed the trail through darkness and snow, wrapped in bear-fur coats. Prinz barked at their heels.

When Walter and Rudi reached Hockalp, they were puffing and panting, for the trail was steep. Many mountain folk stood about a huge pile of logs, hugging themselves to keep warm. They were all very quiet. The dark forest rose about them. The night was crystal clear with the stars like diamonds. Walter found Marie and her grandfather together. The children chased each other and threw snowballs, and so were warm.

Suddenly Walter noticed Klaus, the hermit, standing near. As the boy stopped and stared at him, Klaus knelt in the snow and raised his hands to the sky. Soon all of the herders were kneeling in the snow, even the children. There was a long, long silence as they waited.

And then Klaus prayed, "Dear Lord, Father of all men, look down upon us this great night. Be with us when the bells ring, when the signal fires burn. Help us throw from our shoulders the yoke of the tyrant. But, good Lord, let no blood flow this night in the land of Uri. Even in this, our greatest hour, help us to remember that all men, even evil men, are our brothers. Keep our hearts pure, our arms strong. For the Virgin's sake. Amen."

A deep chorus of "Amens" rose to heaven. And then Walter heard

a sound he had always loved, the deep notes of the great alphorn. Its slow, sad melody rose and fell, echoing from the mountain peaks, growing ever fainter and fainter. Someone played a flute. As the two melodies joined, Walter heard the tolling of distant bells. From far off they came, from valleys below. The bells of Burglen, of Altdorf, of distant Brunnen. Tolling, tolling, deep and sad, they joined with the lovely sounds of alphorn and flute.

"Rudi, listen, it's midnight now. Listen to the bells and the flute and the alphorn." Walter held his brother tightly by the hand. "Look Rudi, they're going to light the fires now, look!"

As the boys watched, little flames like orange flowers blossomed at the base of the woodpile. The flames grew larger. Then all at once a red tongue of fire roared up into the dark sky. The children ran from the fire and held their hands before their faces.

"Look, Marie, look, Rudi, at the other fires," shouted Walter. All about them now on the highest mountain meadows, danced fires, here, there, everywhere.

"Are they going to burn down the mountains?" asked Rudi, frightened of the many fires he saw all about him.

"Of course not, Rudi, don't be scared. The mountains can't burn down, they're wet with ice and snow," soothed Walter.

Now began singing. To the sounds of the flute, the deep alphorn and the distant bells, the people held hands and marched slowly around the fire. They sang an ancient song. It seemed to Walter as he listened that it was a song such as patriots might sing as they carried upon their shoulders the body of some dead hero. He felt a great joy within him. His throat felt tightened and tears were on his cheeks. Only the tears were those of happiness. For at that moment, Walter Tell, a simple mountain lad, seemed to know why thirty-three men had met on that mountain meadow and had sworn an oath to fight and to die together.

Why his own father had stood so fearlessly before Gessler that autumn day in Altdorf. Why he himself had such faith in his father that he was not afraid of anything, even dying. Now he knew why his mother had wished him to be on the alp that night of nights. He felt this only dimly, but he felt it nevertheless. He knew what the wise have always known, that man lives by faith, and that faith can be stronger than fear. . . .

He marched and sang with the others and his heart was full to bursting. And the bells tolled, the fires blazed, and the stars looked down. He forgot all about Rudi, he was so carried away by the beauty and solemnity of that glorious night.

Then someone shouted, "Look—down in the valley—look!" And as they looked, a sudden flame rose against the dark hills. Walter heard heavy sounds as if a giant blacksmith were hitting an anvil with great hammer blows. "The castle of Zwing-Uri is afire," called one. "The castle of Zwing-Uri is falling. Gessler's castle has been captured."

At the word *Gessler,* the people stopped marching. The flute and the alphorn ceased. Then, as if led by a conductor, the people burst suddenly into song again; a song of joy and triumph and liberation. The mountain folk clung to one another as they sang. Some danced as though they had wings upon their feet. The wind was bitter, the snow icy, yet Walter Tell felt neither tired nor cold. He ran and danced with the others, uplifted by the beauty of the music, and the wonder of this night.

The fires dimmed, but on and on the herdsmen danced and sang. The sky in the east lightened with the promise of day. Then Walter felt Marie tugging at his fur cape. "Walter, where is Rudi? I haven't seen him for a long time."

"Oh, Marie, I forgot him! He was here a little while ago. The music was so beautiful and the dancing, I guess I just forgot. And I promised Mother to watch him too. Let's look for him. He may be asleep somewhere."

The two children left the crowd and began to search for the little boy. They could not find him. Then Walter whistled a call that Prinz knew. The herd dog came bounding to him from a hole in a big pine tree. "There he is over there," shouted Marie, "in that tree, see, Walter."

And there lay Rudi, snuggled like a little squirrel in the hole of the tree. With Prinz for a pillow he had kept warm through the night.

"Rudi, Rudi, wake up boy, you'll freeze," shouted Walter, shaking his brother.

"Where am I?" wailed the little boy, "I'm cold, where am I?"

"On Hockalp, Rudi, and this is the New Year. Come, we must go home and you can get warm in bed."

Taking his brother by the hand, Walter half carried and half dragged Rudi down the slippery trail. The fires faded on the mountaintops. The noise of falling timber ceased. The alphorn stopped its sad music. So did the tender little flute. The people began to wander to their homes. And soon came dawn, the dawn of the year 1291. Switzerland was born.

The next day when William Tell and Grandfather came home, they told the Tell family of their adventures in Altdorf. They said that the bailiffs and their knights had fled the land. The castle of Zwing-Uri was now but a pile of black ashes. They heard that the castle of Underwalden was burned to the ground, too. The tyrants had run away and so Uri, Schwyz and Underwalden were free at last. Yet in all of this turmoil few people had died and little blood had been shed.

And so began the little country of Switzerland. As years, decades and centuries passed, other cantons joined with the three. Today twenty-two cantons form the Swiss Republic which we know.

As the years passed, William Tell became an old man with a white beard. He could no longer climb the mountains to hunt for the chamois and the deer, for his eyes were not so keen as they had once been. He lived in the same hut where he had always lived. Whenever he went to Burglen or Altdorf, the people doffed their hats to him as he walked the cobblestone streets or sat in the inn. The people of his canton knew well that they owed a part of their freedom to brave William Tell and to his son Walter.

Walter Tell grew to be a large man like his father, with great brown arms and a dark beard. He too became skilled with the crossbow. He became a hunter of chamois and deer like his father and knew the best places to find game in the Alpine forests. When the time came for him to marry, he chose Marie as his bride. And as the years passed, two sons and two daughters were born to them. He named the oldest William after his own father.

On cold winter evenings, when the hours passed slowly, Walter and Marie would gather their children around them, and tell them stories of the days when they were young. Often the children asked for the story of Gessler and their grandfather and father. For were not their very own father and grandfather now heroes of Switzerland?

Sometimes Walter would relate the story of how those thirty-three men had met on a mountain meadow and vowed to fight together against their tyrants. Then, just before they went to bed, the girls would plead with their mother to tell them how she, their Uncle Rudi and their own father watched the signal fires burn and heard the bells toll on that now distant dawn of 1291.

And so it happened, since children everywhere like the same stories, that other people told their children the story of William and Walter Tell. It spread from one person to another. Before long people in other lands learned too of the great bowman of Uri. Years passed. Centuries passed. This old story was told by father to sons, by mother to daughters. And now today the story of William Tell is the story of one man's revolt against tyranny. It is just as true now as it was in those old days of the thirteenth century, the story of *The Apple and the Arrow.*

THE END